Ladybird books are widely available, but in case of
difficulty may be ordered by post or telephone from:

Ladybird Books – Cash Sales Department
Littlegate Road Paignton Devon TQ3 3BE
Telephone 0803 554761

A catalogue record for this book is available
from the British Library

Published by Ladybird Books Ltd Loughborough Leicestershire UK

THE
TALE OF
BENJAMIN
BUNNY™

Based on the original and authorized story
by Beatrix Potter
Ladybird Books in association with Frederick Warne

One morning, young Benjamin Bunny sat on a bank, watching the world go by.

Trit-trot, trit-trot! A pony and gig went past. The gig was driven by Mr McGregor and beside him sat Mrs McGregor, wearing her best bonnet.

As soon as they had passed, little
Benjamin Bunny set off with a hop,
skip and a jump to visit his Aunt and
cousins, who lived in a wood at the
back of Mr McGregor's garden.

In the woods, Benjamin almost
tumbled over his cousin Peter, who
was sitting by himself wrapped
in a red cotton handkerchief.
He looked poorly.

"What's the matter?" asked Benjamin.

"I went into Mr McGregor's garden yesterday," sniffed Peter. "He chased me away. When I got home Mama gave me some camomile tea and put me to bed."

Benjamin looked at the red cotton handkerchief.

"Where are your clothes?" he asked.

"I lost them in Mr McGregor's garden," said Peter. "Now the scarecrow is wearing them."

"Let's get them back," said Benjamin.
"Mr and Mrs McGregor have gone out
for the day. Mrs McGregor was
wearing her best bonnet."

"I hope it rains," said Peter Rabbit.

Hand in hand, the little rabbits made
their way to Mr McGregor's garden.
They jumped up onto his wall and
looked down.

There was the scarecrow.

It was dressed with Peter's coat and shoes, topped with an old tam-o-shanter belonging to Mr McGregor.

Benjamin climbed down a pear tree
and reached the garden safely. Peter
fell down head first, but he did not
hurt himself because of the soft,
newly raked soil.

The two little rabbits ran over to the scarecrow. Unfortunately, they left little foot-marks all over the garden beds, especially Benjamin, who was wearing clogs.

Benjamin and Peter rescued Peter
Rabbit's clothes. There had been rain
during the night; the coat was
somewhat shrunk and there was
water in the shoes. Benjamin Bunny
tried on the tam-o-shanter, but it
was too big for him.

Then Benjamin suggested that they fill the red cotton handkerchief with onions as a present for his Aunt.

But Peter wanted to go home. He kept hearing noises. Benjamin, on the contrary, was perfectly at home and ate a lettuce leaf.

Little Benjamin said that
they couldn't climb the pear tree
carrying a load of vegetables. He led
the way boldly to the other end of the
garden. As they walked along, Peter
dropped the onions.

They landed amongst some flower-
pots, and frames and tubs.
Peter and Benjamin scrambled to
pick them up and this is what they
saw round the corner!

Quick as a flash, Benjamin hid himself and Peter and the onions underneath a large basket.

The cat got up and stretched herself. Then she came over to sniff at the basket. Perhaps she liked the smell of onions, because she sat down on top of the basket.

She stayed there for *five* hours!

It was dark inside the basket and the smell of onions was terrible. Soon, Peter Rabbit and little Benjamin began to cry.

At length there was a pitter-patter, pitter-patter. The cat looked up and saw old Mr Bouncer walking along the terrace wall. He was smoking a pipe of rabbit-tobacco and had a little switch in his hand. He was looking for his son.

Mr Bouncer had no opinion whatever
of cats. He jumped off the wall and
landed on the cat. Then he cuffed it
and kicked it into the green-house.

Mr Bouncer locked the green-house
door and came back to the basket. He
took Benjamin out by the ears, giving
him a smack with the switch, and
pulled out his nephew Peter.

Then Mr Bouncer picked up the handkerchief of onions, pulled up a fine young lettuce by the root and marched out of the garden.

When Mr McGregor returned, he was puzzled to see that somebody had been walking all over his garden in a pair of clogs – and the footprints were very, very small!

Also, he could not understand how
the cat had managed to shut herself
up *inside* the green-house, locking the
door from the *outside*.

When Peter got home, his mother
forgave him for being late because
she was glad to see that he had found
his shoes and coat.

And, whilst Peter and his sister Cotton-tail folded up the red cotton handkerchief, Mrs Rabbit strung up the onions and hung them from the kitchen ceiling.